STATE OF VERMONT
DEPARTMENT OF LIBRARIES
NORTHWEST REGIONAL LIBRARY
R   #2
FAIRFAX,   RMONT 05454

VERMONT DEPARTMENT OF LIBRARIES
MIDSTATE REGIONAL LIBRARY
RR #4, BOX 1870
MONTPELIER, VERMONT 05602

WITHDRAWN FROM THE COLLECTION OF
STATE OF VERMONT
DEPARTMENT OF LIBRARIES - MR1
MAY NOT BE SOLD

Charles B. Danforth Library
P.O. Box 204
Barnard, VT 05031
802-234-9408

Text copyright © 1983 by Richard Mabey
Pictures copyright © 1983 by Clare Roberts
Volume copyright © 1983 by Bettina Tayleur Ltd
Oak & Company was first published in Great Britain by Kestrel Books
All rights reserved. No part of this book may be reproduced or utilized in any form or by any
means, electronic or mechanical, including photocopying, recording or by any information
storage and retrieval system, without permission in writing from the Publisher, Greenwillow
Books, a division of William Morrow & Co., Inc., 105 Madison Avenue, New York, NY 10016.

Produced by Bettina Tayleur Ltd
1 Newburgh Street, London W1V 1LH
Typesetting by Rowland Phototypesetting Ltd
Printed in Italy by Amilcare Pizzi s.p.a., Milan
First American Edition

Library of Congress Cataloging in Publication Data
Mabey, Richard, (date)   Oak and company.
Summary: Follows an oak tree and its company of
plants and animals from its beginning as an acorn
to its death 282 years later.
1. Oak—Juvenile literature. 2. Oak—Ecology—
Juvenile literature. 3. Botany—Ecology—Juvenile
literature. [1. Oak. 2. Ecology] I. Roberts, Clare.
II. Title. QK495.F14M33   1982   583'.976   82-15618
ISBN 0-688-01993-5

Oak & Company

Oak & Company

Written by Richard Mabey & Illustrated by Clare Roberts

Greenwillow Books, New York

Felix Gluck
in grateful memory

IF tree families had family trees the oaks would have one of the oldest and grandest of all. There are more than 500 different species, and over the last million years they have spread, in various shapes and forms, over most of the northern half of the earth. There are mountain oaks, swamp oaks, evergreen oaks, weeping oaks, and oaks on windswept cliffs that never reach more than two or three feet in height. One kind in Spain has such a spongy bark that it is used to make cork, so there are soft oaks, too. But for most of us oak means just one kind of tree: the tough, rugged giant that has played such a part in history and legend, and been so important in the woodlands of Europe and North America.

Perhaps we've been unfair to other trees, but the forest oaks deserve their fame. They are hardy, easygoing, and not at all fussy about where they grow. They can reach a great age—even a thousand years, though most are cut down long before this. And they are every bit as tough as they look. Their squat trunks and twisted branches, looking like clenched wooden muscles, can stand up to the worst kinds of weather.

On top of all this, timber cut from oaks is as strong and remarkable as the trees themselves. It is solid and hard-wearing, as good for furniture as it is for firewood. Before the days of steel and concrete it made the frames of houses and ships. If we had to invent a new kind of timber it would be hard to think up anything better.

Yet it isn't just humans who find oaks the most useful of trees. Over the ages a huge number of animals and plants have learned to live off—and in—the oaks. It is tempting to say that a full-grown oak is like a house, but it is really more like a city—a whole community of creatures traveling, working, eating, sleeping, singing, and bringing up young, on every part from the topmost spring buds to the dead gash blasted out by a lightning flash.

This is the story of one great oak, and its company of plants and animals, from its beginning as an acorn to its death. It is the story of a particular tree, but what happens to it will have happened to most oaks allowed to reach their full natural age.

THE Oak's first two leaves unfolded on their matchstick-sized stem on an Easter Sunday at the very beginning of the eighteenth century. That was early in the year for an oak to leaf, but the seedling had sprung up in a warm and sheltered spot by a stream, and had not missed a minute of the spring sunshine.

Its story really began the previous autumn, when its parent tree had produced more than a thousand acorns. It was a good crop, but in late August they were invaded by a swarm of weevils. These little beetles drilled through many of the soft shells to lay their eggs, and when the grubs hatched they set about eating the contents. More acorns were eaten by mice and squirrels. Others fell into a damp hollow, became mildewed, and began to rot away. Less than a hundred survived to put down roots, and most of these were under the shade of their parent tree and would never have enough light to grow.

But none of these oakling deaths really mattered. In the end only one sapling needed to survive to take the place of the parent tree. The streamside Oak looked set to be the lucky one right from the start. The acorn from which it grew had been carried out of the wood by a jay, then dropped and forgotten in a patch of rough ground. Its first leaves had opened under a protective cover of thorn scrub, safe from hungry and inquisitive cattle. Throughout that first, fine summer these leaves grew food for the sapling, and on its first birthday the Oak was thirteen inches tall. By the end of its fifth year it had reached six feet, and was bristling with leafy side twigs.

It was now being visited by dozens of feeding creatures, greenflies and sawflies that bored into the leaves to suck the sap—and warblers and titmice that came in turn to snap up the flies.

The Oak had also begun to grow its first gall. One of its leaf stalks was swelling where a wasp had laid its eggs. By midwinter the swelling looked like a small, wrinkled apple. Over the years many kinds of gall wasp laid their eggs in different parts of the Oak, and galls of all kinds appeared, some like tiny buttons under the leaves and some like bunches of currants on the catkins.

DESPITE all this chewing of leaves and sucking of sap, the young Oak wasn't too troubled by its visitors. While it had been growing in the shelter of the thorn scrub it had developed deep roots that were full of stored food—enough for the Oak to grow a whole new set of leaves if necessary.

But its cousins, growing on shaded and almost bare ground inside the wood, had not been so lucky. Every spring their juicy leaves, and often their whole stems, were eaten away by rabbits and pigeons. Many died before they were a year old. Those that survived had to face more plagues later in the summer, when thousands of leaf-eating caterpillars parachuted down from the larger trees on silken threads and set to work on their last tattered leaves. By the time our Oak was in its seventh winter only two young trees from its acorn year were still alive.

The Oak was now beginning to outgrow the thorn scrub, and it had its own problems. Its branches spread wide enough to be reached by cattle and deer, which promptly browsed them back level with the thorn. And one winter when farm workers came to trim back the scrub on their grazing land, they did not notice the Oak and sliced off its top only four feet above the ground. This was the worst calamity that had so far befallen the Oak. But it did not die. Its deep roots had saved its life, and by the next spring two strong new shoots were beginning to grow skyward where there had been just one before.

Over the next forty years the Oak grew into a sizable tree, but for the rest of its life it had an unusual pair of twin trunks, the mark of that accident in its seventh year. The larger it became, the more other plants and creatures were able to find somewhere to live in it. On the damp upper surfaces of the branches, and in crevices of the bark where rotting leaves collected, ferns and mosses grew from wind-borne spores. A thread of honeysuckle began to climb into the lowest branches. Butterflies fed among the sunlit leaves, woodpeckers searched for insects among the mosses, and other birds nested in the shade.

The Oak was becoming a community. It was also becoming an adult, and in its forty-ninth year it produced its first crop of acorns.

WHEN the Oak reached its first century, it was over sixty feet high, and two people could only just join hands around the trunk. Nearly an inch was added to its girth every year, as new green wood grew just under the bark. And every year an earlier year's green wood dried out and joined the tough heartwood in the center of the tree.

If the Oak had been cut down we would have seen a cross section of these rings, and the way in which they varied in shape and thickness each year. Counting their number would have told us the Oak's age, but their pattern was a record of its whole history, of droughts and insect plagues and winter disasters. Close to the center, for instance, we would have seen the very thin ring added the summer after the Oak's top was sliced off. That year all its food reserves had gone toward building up a new set of branches and leaves, and there had been little to spare for the trunk.

This wood in the center of the tree was dead, but it was still vital to the Oak. It formed a kind of skeleton, or inside scaffolding, and kept the tree sturdy and upright. The living parts of the trunk were the newest rings of wood under the bark. Every day the innermost of these drew up many gallons of water through the roots and pumped them to the leaves. There the green chemical chlorophyll did its miraculous job of using sunlight to turn air and water into sugary sap, which then flowed down through the outermost ring of green wood to feed other parts of the tree.

The bark itself acted like a skin, and kept molds and fungi away from the heartwood. When gales occasionally snapped off branches close to the trunk, new wood grew over the scars and formed dome-shaped burrs. But one year a broken branch took with it a long tongue of bark. The wound did not heal, the wood dried, and a woodpecker drilled out a nest-hole in it. Some years later, as more dry wood broke off, the hole became big enough for an owl, first to roost, then to bring up a brood of three young.

The owls weren't alone. Into the nest-hole drifted fungus spores, then ants and beetles that fed off dead wood. The first chink had been made in the Oak's armor.

WHEN it was close on 120 years old, the number of plants and animals in the Oak's company began to overtake its age in years. There were squirrels and jays in the topmost branches; mosses, ferns, lichens, and even a sprig of mistletoe using the branches as a base; two kinds of woodpecker nesting in holes in the trunk; and all manner of insects scrounging a living in every conceivable part of the tree—under flakes of bark, in the jagged ends of broken branches, deep inside buds and acorns, and even in the pool of water that had collected between the two main trunks and proved much to the liking of a colony of mosquitoes.

There were almost as many creatures living under the ground, amongst the Oak's roots. The roots were like a mirror image of the tree: they spread as wide as the branches, and in places were almost as thick. Some minute worms known as nematodes spent their lives inside the roots. Other creatures browsed on the hairlike tendrils that grew out of the main stems. There were even oak apples swelling on parts of the root.

None of these creatures interfered very much with the roots' job of taking water and nourishment from the soil. Some—including several plants—actually helped. Entwined amongst the roots, for instance, were the long white threads that make up the underground part of fungi. They are known as mycelia; what we call toadstools are really just fruits of the fungus. The fungus and the Oak roots lived in a kind of partnership, the fungus swapping some of the nourishing chemicals it was able to extract from decaying leaves in the soil for the sugary foods which the Oak made in its leaves.

In amongst all this underground activity larger animals went about their business. Wood mice and rabbits hollowed out homes under the big roots near the surface. And one winter a large and energetic fox moved into one of the burrows and began scratching out an earth, which soon stretched right underneath the tree.

BY now the Oak was as tall as a small church. It was a mighty structure to keep fed and watered, and produced a huge amount of refuse. Every year enough plant litter fell from it to cram a dozen trash cans full. There were twigs, bark, and scraps of fungus blown down in winter, bud scales, catkins, and young shoots in the spring, and throughout the late summer and autumn hundreds of thousands of leaves and acorns. Added to this was the litter from all those creatures that lived on the Oak: galls, chrysalis cases, dead insects that had once munched the leaves—and the droppings of birds that had eaten the insects.

Very little of this was wasted. Some of the fresher litter—especially green acorns and young leaves—was carried off by deer and squirrels on feeding expeditions from the nearby wood, but most stayed where it fell. It became part of the layer of decaying plant matter, known as humus, which had begun to build up under the Oak after its first autumn. This was the soil in which the Oak grew, from which it took its nourishment. It was a kind of food bank—saving the goodness from the litter and paying it out to the roots.

And helping to break down the litter, so that it could be useful again, was another whole branch of the Oak's company. These were the scavengers, animals that lived off dead and decaying matter. There were more than twenty million of them living in the soil under the shade of the Oak, and they ranged from slugs, snails, and wood lice grazing on fallen leaves on the surface, to millipedes, centipedes, beetles, caterpillars, and ants, down to countless tiny microbes. Among the most important were the earthworms. Nearly a million lived under the Oak, and they spent much of their time eating through the litter, swallowing leaves and rough earth, and leaving behind them the trails of fine soil known as casts.

The worms acted like small plows, turning over and blending the soil. They also helped create air channels, which gave the roots of smaller plants room to grow. Already a few delicate woodland flowers—anemones, wood sorrel, bluebells—that needed shady, un-farmed ground to prosper had moved in from the wood and begun to spread.

MOST years woodmen came to harvest some of the oaks. The Oak by the stream was not on their land and they never touched it. But they often cut trees in the wood, and one spring they felled an acre of oaks that included the Oak's parent. Although this tree might well have lived twice as long as its 200 years, its timber was at its best now, and the huge lower branches were shading out and slowing the growth of nearby trees.

The woodmen planned to sell its wood to a furniture maker, and some of the younger trees for making roof rafters. But they were just as interested in the stumps that were left, for cutting down the trunks of young oaks didn't kill them. Under the ground their bundles of roots, full of food and moisture stored up from the previous year's sun and rain, began to come to life as the spring sunshine warmed up the soil. Within a few weeks of the felling, the parent oak's stump had begun to form a ring of new buds, just below the bark. By June they had put out a sheaf of straight new shoots eighteen inches tall.

Ten years later these shoots would have grown into tall, straight poles, and they would be cut again. Some would be used as firewood, some as rungs for ladders and chair legs. The oak went on producing new poles after each cut, and its base grew gradually broader just as if it were growing as a single trunk.

For the streamside Oak, the spring its parent tree was felled went by much like any other. The yellowish young leaves began to break from the bud at the end of April and great numbers, as usual, were eaten by caterpillars before they had a chance to reach their full size. In the middle of May the flowers appeared—tiny female stars and pale green male catkins, some of which were host to currant galls. But one thing was different this year. Toward the end of May a strong, warm breeze kept up for several days, and pollen from all the oaks along the stream was blown about and mixed. That week some of the Oak's female flowers were reached for the first time by pollen from a tree downstream, the tallest and straightest oak in the district.

SOMETIMES the oak poles were cropped more for their bark than their wood, and then the cutting went on into early summer, when the sap running in the green wood made the bark easy to peel off. Oak bark is rich in a chemical called tannin (also found in wine and tea!) which is used to soften and preserve animal hides so that they can be used as leather. Poles of about ten years' growth were preferred, and their bark was stripped off in June to be sent by horse cart to the leather-tanning works.

No one is sure why oaks contain so much tannin. But it may be part of their natural defenses, and may "cure" the living parts of the tree and protect them from attacks by insects and fungus just as it cures and preserves leather.

As summer drew on, the amount of tannin in the Oak rose, until by the end of July there was so much that even the leaves became too bitter for some insects to eat. This was just as well, because by this time in the year the Oak was already into its second set of leaves. The first growth had been chewed away by the thousands of small green caterpillars that swarmed about the tree during the spring. These new leaves were tinged a beautiful reddish color, and were known as Lammas shoots after Lammas Day, August 1st.

One late summer, when it was more than 160 years old, the Oak was struck by lightning. The flash burned a long deep scar in the bark of one of the Oak's twin trunks—the other was already damaged where branches had been broken off. By early autumn the first fungus spores had reached the damp, charred wood. The second breach in the Oak's defenses had been made.

But only a hundred yards away, one of its descendants was already shaping up to be one of the most handsome trees in the valley. It had sprung from that chance mixing of pollens nearly forty years before, and straight-trunked, high-branching, and decked out in its own Lammas shoots, would prove a worthy successor to the Oak.

AUTUMN was harvesttime, and round the oaks, too, there was a great gathering-in of crops. Acorns were the favorites. They were such tidy and compact parcels of food, meant to give young oaks a start in life, after all, that almost everything that crawled or walked or flew was after them. Beetles bored into their shells. Squirrels gnawed their tops off, sitting on their haunches and turning them round in their front paws. Woodpeckers, too, occasionally took a few, wedging them in oak bark grooves while they hammered them open. Jays ferried them away for another day and sometimes forgot all about them.

Not so many centuries before, humans, too, had eaten the acorns. It was a long and bothersome business preparing them, but worth the trouble when food was short in the winter. The acorns had to be shelled, ground up, washed through with hot water to take out the bitterness, and then used as a rough kind of flour. Now farmers fed the acorns to pigs and ate bacon instead! Every three or four years, when there was an especially good crop of acorns, the pigs were allowed to roam about in the streamside pastures, and sometimes in parts of the wood where there were no young saplings or tender shoots. The pigs made a great mess grubbing about in the ground, but this buried many of the acorns and meant that they had a better chance of sprouting into new oaklings the following spring.

There were other harvests under the trees, including the shiny brown toadstools known as cepes that grew from white tendrils entwined with the Oak's roots. They looked like small buns, but tasted a little like soft hazel nuts.

Not everything was gathered in as food, however. The undersides of many of the Oak's leaves were covered with tiny spangle galls, each one containing a wasp larva. As the leaves began to shrivel, these galls fell to the ground, and just a few days later the leaves themselves fell and buried them. So the galls spent the winter under cover, safe from hungry birds until the wasps hatched out in the spring.

THE wear and tear of two hundred winters left their mark on the Oak. Winds racing down the valley every January twisted and snapped the branches and gave the whole tree a tilt toward the south. In one fierce storm the tree was struck by lightning again, and the top branches were set on fire. Dry oak burns well. Everyone knew that, and when cold weather set in the local people would come down to the stream to lop branches from the oaks for firewood.

At this moment of the year, with all its leaves fallen, the Oak looked as much like a pillar of rock as a tree. It was pitted with holes and grooves, and patches of spongy, rotting wood. There was no other tree in the valley that looked quite like it, and people used it as a landmark, a place to meet and chat and sometimes picnic under. The younger children used to imagine they could see heads and faces in it, and in the half-light of a winter's evening it was not difficult to turn some of those knots and gaping holes into eyes and mouths.

In these cold months the Oak was a great gathering ground for birds and animals, too. An owl roosted in the largest hole, and a dormouse snoozed away the winter in a mossy nest built deep inside the trunk. On the most bitter nights, when the ground was iron hard and the Oak's trunk was encased in a film of ice, the birds stopped being wary of each other. If you had watched the Oak at dusk, you might have seen more than twenty titmice fly into one of its hollow branches to spend the night huddled together for warmth.

Of course they would feed when they could, picking out sleeping grubs from the bark, bringing berries to eat in the shelter of the upper branches and often leaving the seeds there with their droppings, caught in one of the damp leaf-filled crevices. And that is how a miniature forest of thorn, holly, and currant bushes came to grow more than fifteen feet above the ground, rooted not in the earth, but in the Oak—a wood inside a tree!

A FEW years after it had been struck by lightning again, the Oak began to age quickly. Channels of rotting wood had begun to eat away both of its trunks, and these spread and joined up. The following spring the heavier of the two—almost half the tree—broke off in a spring gale. The Oak was now in desperate straits. It had lost half its food-producing leaves, and was riddled with holes and gashes in constant need of repair. It put out new twigs near the break, but the space left by its fallen branches had already been filled with new foliage from younger trees. As more and more of its branches were shaded out, so the roots which they fed died. At the same time the healthy roots were being weakened by the underground burrowings of rabbits and foxes.

One winter night in its 283rd year, the Oak was hit by a blizzard. Freezing snow drifted on what was left of its upper branches, until the remaining roots could take the weight and strain no longer. They snapped, and were wrenched out of the ground as the tree fell: the second twin trunk split off, slewed round and crashed through the telegraph wires that now ran alongside the stream.

That was why the fallen Oak was discovered only hours later. The foresters dealt with it very quickly, using chain saws to free the wires.

There were too many crooks and hollows for the timber to be of any use, but the foresters did save the burr which had formed over a broken branch more than a hundred years before, because of the beautiful grain patterns the green wood had made growing back over the scar. The rest of the tree they left to rot. So even after its death, the Oak was still host to dozens of toadstools and insects.

Much has happened along the valley in the few years since the Oak's death. Self-sown oak trees—including the Oak's own offspring—have grown into a small wood along the stream. The farmers want this felled so that they will have more land for grazing. The owner of the wood where the Oak's parent grew (now growing spruce trees, not oaks) wants to extend his Christmas tree plantation down to the stream. But one forester has seen the straight trunks of the Oak's descendants and wants them left, to see if they will make a new strain of timber oaks.

The Oak's great company, the woodpeckers and butterflies, the mosses and beetles, have moved to these younger oaks, and wait to see what the future will bring.

583.9
Mab

DATE DUE

Mabey, R
Oak & Company

Charles B. Danforth Library
P.O. Box 204
Barnard, VT 05031
802-234-9408

DEMCO